Dark Shadows
RL: 10 – 11y

This book is one of many in the "Choose a Path" series. Each "Choose a Path" book is accompanied by specially recorded audio support and activities that are fun and educational.

"Choose a Path" books put the reader in charge of making choices and experiencing the consequences of their decisions. There are multiple paths to follow with multiple endings; encouraging the research-proven technique of repeated readings.

©Pikopiko Publishing Ltd. 2012
P.O. Box 561, Nelson
New Zealand
www.chooseapathbooks.com
ISBN: 978-1-927188-03-3

Choose A Path

You're about to start a "Choose a Path" book. The main character in this story is you!

Your adventure starts on page 2, then continues wherever you choose to go. The choices you make will take you on many exciting, mysterious and sometimes dangerous adventures. The good news is, at any stage, you can return to make different choices which lead to new adventures.

You can keep track of your adventures, using the Journey Log at the back of the book or printed from the Activity Disk. You can also write some different choices of your own.

With "Choose a Path" the choices are yours!

This "Choose a Path" book is called ...

DARK SHADOWS

MERYL-LYNN PLUCK

Illustrated by Peter Lole

The year is 1855.
You're living with your family on Flores Island, off the coast of Portugal.

One cold evening you're sitting at home by the fire, reading.

Your mother's cooking dinner. She says to you, "We need some milk. Would you go to the farm and get us a bucket of milk, please? Take some money from the tin."

You feel annoyed at all the boring chores you're expected to do. You wish your life was more exciting. You long for adventure. You get up off the floor and snatch your coat off the hook.

It's getting dark outside and, although you crave adventure, you're more than a bit nervous at the thought of being out alone in the dark.

Evil things have been happening in your village. You live in a fishing port and bad sailors often visit. You know of people who have gone missing. Others have been physically attacked, some even killed.

You open the door and look outside. It's not quite dark but there are dark shadows on the path. You look up and down the street and try to swallow your fear. Although it's just a five-minute run to the farm, the walk home will be slow with a bucket full of milk. You really don't want to go outside, but you're the oldest in your family. Your father's not home from work yet and your mother's busy.

If you choose to tell your mother you're too scared to go out,
go to page 9.

If you choose to be brave and go to get the milk,
go to page 29.

You want excitement and adventure, so you choose to join the men in the whaleboat.

It's not long before you hear the call, "Thar she blows!" There's a frenzy of activity as the ship is turned towards a whale that's been sighted. The sails are adjusted and the whaleboats are lowered into the ocean. Each whaleboat is manned by six crew. There are four oarsmen, including you, a harpooner and a sailor who steers.

You row like crazy to get close to the whale.

The harpooner throws the harpoon which is attached to the boat by a three-hundred metre rope. The harpoon hits the whale in the heart and the whale swims away, taking you, in the whaleboat, off at terrific speed.

'This is the excitement and adventure I've been craving,' you think with a smile.

THE END

You decide you really must get off the ship quickly, before it sets sail.

You rush out of the bunk room and up the stairs to the main deck. The deck is crowded with sailors all busily preparing sails to hoist.

There's a gigantic cooking pot over to your left. It smells like the oil you use at home to fuel your lanterns. You crouch down beside it while you catch your breath.

You wonder if you should ask someone to help you or if you should try to get off the ship without being seen.

A sailor walks close by.

*If you choose to ask the sailor to help you, **go to page 31**.*

If you choose to make a dash for the gangplank,
go to page 27.

You believe life on board a whaling ship may be bearable now you have a friend. You push thoughts of your family out of your head.

"OK," you say. "Show me the ropes! I've seen the bunk room."

"Follow me," says the sailor and he takes you on a guided tour.

He shows you where the lookouts stand on the cross-stays (two wooden rungs at the top of the main mast) searching for a sight of whales.

"This is a good job," says the sailor, "as you earn extra rations each time you spot a whale. We don't get a lot to eat so any extras are always welcome. You'd be best to avoid the whaleboats – the work is tiring and dangerous. A lot of men get injured from ropes, harpoons or whales."

The sailor's stories make you feel nervous but excited and pleased that you decided to stay.

THE END

The men look up and see you. One whispers something to the other. They start running towards you. You turn and run. You're a fast runner and expect to be able to outrun them. You glance over your shoulder and to your horror you see they're closer than they were before. You stumble and a stab of pain shoots up your ankle. You hobble and the men get even closer. They're now close enough for you to hear them calling.

"Stop. We won't hurt you. We just want to talk to you."

You don't know whether to believe them. You do know you can't run very fast with a sore ankle. There's a house up ahead. You wonder if you'd be safer going to the stranger's house or stopping to talk to the men.

*If you choose to run into the house, **go to page 17.***
If you choose to stop and talk to the men,
go to page 10.

8

You brush the dirt off your clothes.

You notice your sleeve is torn. This makes you furious.

You think of the hungry baby at home and this makes you even angrier.

How dare people rob others of their money? You decide the only thing to do is go to the police.

Yes, it's dark. Yes, there are evil people about, but you're not going to let the men get away with robbery.

You make your way to the police station and tell them your story.

A kind policeman thanks you for the information and takes you home. Together, you stop on the way to get milk for the baby. Your mother pays the policeman for the milk and he tells your mother how courageous you've been.

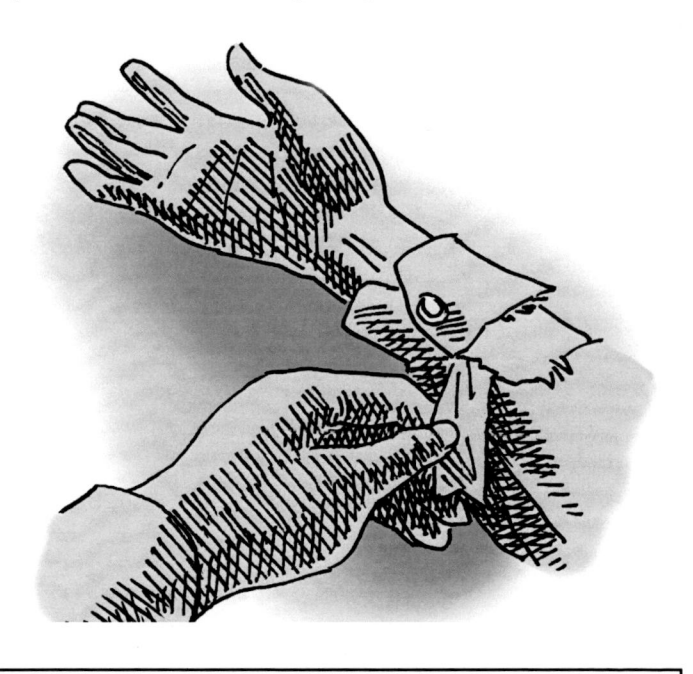

THE END

"It's getting dark outside," you tell your mother. "I'm too scared to go out alone."

"We're almost out of milk," your mother says.

"But there are wicked people about. My friend's father went missing last week."

"We don't know if he was taken against his will," says your mother. "He sometimes chooses to go away for a week or two then returns."

"But he didn't take any clothes this time," you point out.

"If you hurry, you'll be back before it's really dark," your mother says.

"Do we really need milk tonight?" you ask.

"Yes, the baby needs milk before she goes to sleep for the night," says your mother. "Ask your brother to go with you, if you're nervous."

If you choose to ask your brother to go with you,
go to page 15.

If you choose to go out in the dark by yourself,
go to page 29.

10

Your ankle is now throbbing. You doubt you can walk much further and you certainly can't run. You slow down and the men catch up with you.

"What do you want to talk to me about?" you ask, nervously.

"We're sailors," one of them says. "The captain of our ship has asked us to find some young people who'd like an adventure at sea. The pay's great and we have lots of good times."

Both men smile. You notice they're quite young; not much older than you.

'Adventure with great pay and good times,' you think.
This sounds like fun!

Go to page 22.

You've never heard of New Zealand or Australia. They sound a bit too adventurous, even for you.

"I'd prefer America," you say.

You're pushed roughly up the gangplank of the second ship.

You're handed a small bundle of clothing, then pushed down some stairs and into a small, smelly bunk room.
Eight hammocks hang close together.

In one of the hammocks a sailor is moaning in agony.

"What's wrong?" you ask.

"I was late for duty two days running," says the sailor.
"My punishment was the whip … twenty lashes on my bare back. The wounds went rotten. There are no ointments or medicines on board."

Hearing this makes you have second thoughts about adventure and excitement.

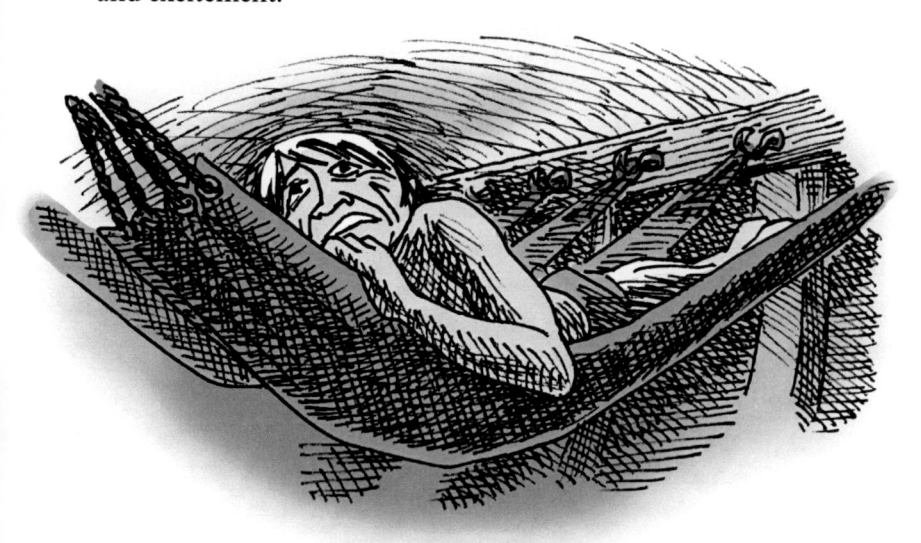

*If you choose to stay but keep out of trouble, **go to page 23**.*
If you choose to try and escape before the ship sets sail,
go to page 5.

12

You turn left and take the path past the well-lit houses.

You can see inside people's homes.

You can see children playing and women cooking meals.

You can see a man reading a newspaper. You smile and think how silly you were to feel afraid. If you were to shout, there would be plenty of people around to hear you.

You just come into view of the farm gate when suddenly you hear a noise behind you.

You see the dark shadows of two men as one grabs you. A filthy hand goes over your mouth. You try to shout but the hand stops any noise escaping. You're dragged into a cluster of bushes. Your coins are ripped out of your hand.

A voice says, "Don't even think of going to the police."

Then the men run away. Your heart is beating madly but you're not badly hurt.

If you choose to make a run for home, **go to page 25.**
*If you choose to go to the police station
and report the robbery,* **go to page 8.**

"OK," you say. "The big red glass marble can be yours, but hurry as it's getting darker by the second."

John pulls his trousers on over his pyjama pants and puts on his coat.

You get some coins from the money tin and open the door.

"Race you there," John calls as he runs past you.

You both arrive at the farmer's door at the same time. You pay for the milk.

Together you carry the bucket home, slowly and carefully so you don't spill any milk. You hear noises in the bushes. You see dark shadows of strangers scurrying around. You're grateful you're not alone. You open your front door and gladly give John your big red glass marble.

THE END

14

"I don't want to be here," you shout.

"I was shanghaied, kidnapped, taken against my will. My parents don't know where I am. I want to go home!"

"Right, it's the cupboard for you," says a sailor.

"You'll be tied up and put in a tiny cupboard teeming with cockroaches. You'll be fed a single sea biscuit and water twice a day, if you're remembered. You won't see any daylight for at least seven days."

"Then what'll happen?" you ask in a small frightened voice.

"You'll be handed over to the police at the next port of call. They'll be informed you're a stowaway. You'll be punished severely and sent home, if you're lucky."

The thought of home sounds good to you, so you hold your arms out so they can be tied together.

THE END

"John," you say. "Fancy a trip to the farm with me to get milk for the baby?"

"I'm in my pyjamas," he says.

"You could put your clothes on over the top," you suggest.

"I'm practising a new trick with my marbles," he says.

"We'll just be fifteen minutes," you say.

"You're scared!" John says. "I'll come if I can have your big red glass marble."

Your heart sinks.

Your big red glass marble is your pride and joy.

*If you choose to give the marble to John so he'll go with you to get the milk, **go to page 13**.*

*If you choose to tell him no, you'll go by yourself and keep your marble, **go to page 18**.*

16

You look around you, searching for somewhere to hide.

You breathe a sigh of relief when you see a large bush close by.

The men are still pushing each other and shouting.

They don't appear to have seen you. You dive into the bushes and lie very still. As the men get closer you can hear their conversation.

They're talking about robbing a bank. One man is arguing that they should break into the bank tonight, under the cover of darkness. The other man is saying it would be easier to do it tomorrow when the bank's open.

The men pass by. They don't know you've heard their plans.

You lie very still wondering what to do.

*If you choose to run home, **go to page 30.***

If you choose to tell the police what you heard,
go to page 8.

17

Your parents have warned you about talking to strange men.

They've also warned you about the dangers of going into the houses of strangers.

Then you recall the stories of people who've been abducted. Some have been hurt, some even killed. They've all been out on the streets after dark. You decide you'll probably be safer in the strange house.

You run up the front path and knock loudly on the door.

The door opens just a crack and a woman's voice asks if she can help you.

You tell her you believe you're being chased. She pulls you inside and locks the door. She gives you a hot drink, then her husband goes with you to the farm. You get the milk for the baby and the kind man walks you safely home.

THE END

"Forget it," you tell your brother.

"I'm not giving away my big red glass marble. I'd rather go for the milk by myself."

"Suit yourself," he says. "But watch out for the robbers and murderers."

"I can run faster than any robbers and murderers," you say.

"Even when you're carrying a bucket of milk?" he asks.

"Sure!" you say, managing to sound braver than you feel.

You get some coins from the money tin and head out onto the dark street.

You get to the corner of the street and stop.

You have two paths to choose from. One path is longer than the other but it would take you past houses that are well lit. The other path is shorter and quicker but would take you through a dark forest.

*If you choose to take the long well-lit path, **go to page 12**.*

*If you choose to take the short dark path, **go to page 32**.*

The thought of a dark cupboard is worse than the thought of working. At least you'll see daylight if you work. And you'll be paid. You can keep on the lookout for a chance to escape. It could even be fun. You were looking for adventure, after all.

"I'll work," you say.

"Good," says the officer. "This is a whaling boat. We hunt whales. You have two choices of where to work. The cook needs a kitchen hand. You'd work below deck. You'd be well fed. The work's easy but boring and it's dark and smelly down in the galley. The other choice is up on the deck as a deckhand; mainly cleaning. You'd get plenty of fresh air and sunlight but the work's hard. It can also be dangerous as the sailors are very rough and mean."

If you choose the safe, boring work in the galley,
go to page 23.

If you choose the work up on the deck, **go to page 20.**

You're feeling a bit seasick. You can't stand the idea of working with food, in the dark, below deck.

"I'll work on the deck," you say.

"Right," says the officer. "I'll show you your bunk. Not that you'll spend much time in it," he laughs. "You'll report to the main deck at 0600 hours every morning. You'll do everything asked of you by any officer. You'll work sixteen hours every day, but only eight hours on Sundays. You'll get a fifteen minute break every four hours. Keep out of trouble because the punishments are harsh!"

And you thought you had it tough at home!

"Your first job's waiting for you over there," says the officer. "A whale has just been pulled aboard and there's blood all over the deck. Start scrubbing!"

The thought of blood turns your stomach.

*If you choose to start scrubbing, **go to page 21**.*
*If you choose to refuse to do the scrubbing, **go to page 28**.*

21

With a heavy heart and heaving stomach, you pick up a scrubbing brush and bucket. You fill the bucket with water from the sea. You start scrubbing and the water turns red immediately.

It's dangerous work, especially as the deck gets slippery.

You turn around at the sound of a rough, mocking voice.

"We have ourselves a new deck rat." A foot kicks over your bucket of water.

You remember the officer's warning: "Keep out of trouble because the punishments are harsh!"

"Yes, I'm the new deckhand," you announce cheerfully and extend your hand.

The sailor hesitates, then breaks into a smile and shakes your hand.

"The name's Scar," he says. "Welcome aboard. Anyone gives you trouble, you tell me!"

'Phew!' you think. 'They're not all as mean as they look, but roll on next port of call and my chance to get off this stinking ship.'

THE END

"Where's the ship going?" you ask. "What kind of work would I do? How much would I get paid?"

"So many questions," says the younger of the two men. "Come back to the ship with us and meet the captain. He'll answer your questions."

"I should discuss it with my parents," you say.

"Bad idea!" says the older man and thrusts a cloth over your nose. It smells terrible. It hurts your throat and it makes you feel sleepy.

You try to struggle, but your arms and legs won't move.

You wake hours later and realise you're on a ship at sea.

You hear a voice saying, "You have two choices. You can work and be paid for your work. Or you can be tied up and placed in a cupboard. If you choose that option you'll be dropped ashore at the next port."

*If you choose to work, **go to page 19.***
*If you choose to be tied up and put in a cupboard until the ship gets to the next port, **go to page 14.***

You go down to the galley. Standing at a sink with his back to you is a very large tattooed man.

You introduce yourself and tell him you'd like to be his kitchen hand.

"Good," says the cook. "I can do with as much help as I can get. The sailors are always hungry." He looks you up and down.

"You look hungry yourself. Help yourself to a pot of stew off the fire. It's horse meat. Make the most of it while we have fresh meat. In a couple of days there'll be nothing but fish; mainly whale."

As you eat, the cook tells you the rules.

"You'll report to the kitchen every morning at 0600 hours. You'll do everything asked of you by any officer. You'll work sixteen hours every day, except Sundays when you'll work eight. You'll get a fifteen minute break every four hours. Keep out of trouble because the punishments are harsh!"

And you thought you had a lot of chores at home!

THE END

Just ten minutes ago you'd been wishing your life was more exciting. You'd been longing for adventure. The men who captured you are big and strong. They are watching you and there is no way you are going to be able to get away from them. You decide to cooperate.

"I'll go on the ship bound for the South Pacific Ocean, please," you say.

"Good choice," is the reply and you're pushed up the gangplank of a ship.

Within seconds you hear the call, "Setting sail in five minutes!"

You start looking around you.

You're hungry and follow your nose to the kitchen.

You introduce yourself to the cook.

"I heard there's a good job on offer," says the cook.

"It's in the whaleboat; harpooning whales. It's really exciting but also very dangerous. It's not too late to go home if you want to. I'll help you, if that's your choice."

*If you choose to harpoon whales, **go to page 4**.*

*If you choose to go home, **go to page 26**.*

25

You pick yourself up off the ground.

Your clothes are torn. Your milk money has gone.

The police station is at least ten minutes away and there could be more danger lurking on the dark streets.

The robber may be watching you and he warned you not to go to the police. You decide the best option is to go home.

You head for home but first call into your neighbour's house. You tell them what happened and they give you some milk for the baby.

Your mother hugs you when you tell her what happened. She gives you an extra big serving of stew. Your brother looks shocked and gives you his best marble.

THE END

"I really do need to go home," you say. "My family will be wondering where I am. I left home an hour ago to get some milk for the baby. She needs it before her bedtime. If you could help me escape, I'd be very grateful."

A hand points to a hiding place near the gangplank at the stern of the ship. You whisper your thanks and cautiously head towards it.

You crouch behind a bag of ropes when you hear voices.

The voices fade and you make a dash for the gangplank.

You make your way ashore and run all the way to the farm, without stopping.

Your father's there, worried about your disappearance.

You tell him about your narrow escape as you go together to buy milk to take home to the baby.

"Home," you say to your father. "Boring but safe!"

Your father smiles, hugs you close and nods in agreement.

THE END

You decide to make a dash for the gangplank and hope everyone's too busy to see you.

You take a moment to look around and confirm this is no place for you. It's dirty and smelly. You can see cockroaches and rats. The men are noisy and swearing. The thought of staying on board terrifies you.

You creep towards the gangplank, looking this way and that.

It's clear the ship is about to set sail, so you need to hurry.

You make it to the gangplank and decide to run.

A voice calls, "Runaway!"

You run faster and don't look back.

You make it to the farm and buy the milk.

You arrive home relieved. Boring is good. You've had enough adventure and excitement in one evening to last you a lifetime!

THE END

Your stomach does an extra big churn and you swallow hard.

"I can't stand the sight of blood, sir," you say.

"I suggest you get used to it then," says the officer.

"Sorry, but I simply can't and won't."

"Then you give me no choice," says the officer. "Bring me the cat-o'-nine-tails!"

Your sick stomach clenches with fear as the officer is handed a whip. Your shirt is ripped off your back. The whip slashes your back once, twice, three times. The pain is unbearable but the whip keeps slashing. You lose count after ten lashings.

The officer throws a scrubbing brush at you and says cruelly, "Let's see if you can stand the sight of blood now!"

Go to page 21.

"I'll go," you say.

"Thanks," says your mother. "When your father gets home, I'll send him to meet you."

You get some coins from the money tin and pick up the bucket.

You open the door, step outside and take a deep breath.

You walk down the street, listening for noises. You look all around you, ready to run if you spot danger.

As you turn a corner you see up ahead of you two dark shadows.

You look more carefully and see the dark shadows belong to two men.

They're shouting and pushing each other.

They make you feel nervous and you don't want to go past them.

If you choose to hide until the men have gone past,
go to page 16.

If you choose to run past the men as fast as you can,
go to page 7.

You peek out from the bush to make sure the men are nowhere in sight.

You crawl out and dust yourself off. You take a deep breath and run for home. You see a man coming towards you. You stop running and wonder what to do. Then you hear your father's voice, calling your name.

You've never been so pleased to see him.

"No milk yet?" he asks.

You tell him what happened and what you heard. He says it needs to be reported to the police.

First you go together to buy some milk from the farm.
You take it home for your mother to give to the baby. Then you both make your way to the police station. No time for dinner. A robbery needs to be stopped!

THE END

"Excuse me," you whisper. There's so much noise on the deck the sailor doesn't hear you.

You clear your throat loudly and the sailor looks over your way.

You notice he's about your age. Hopefully he'll help you.

"I wonder if you could help me," you say. "I was shanghaied."

The sailor looks puzzled.

"I was kidnapped. I don't want to be here. I want to go home to my family. Would you help me?"

"Sure," says the sailor. "The same happened to me. I was living in Italy. I didn't like life on the whaling ship to begin with. I was homesick, but now I like the adventure and excitement. I reckon you might grow to like it. How about giving it a go?"

*If you choose to go home, **go to page 26.***

*If you choose to try life as a sailor on a whaling ship,
go to page 6.*

You choose the short path, thinking the quicker you can get home the better.

You head off through the forest. The tall trees cast long dark shadows. You're frightened when you hear strange noises.

Suddenly a man jumps out in front of you.

You turn around, planning to run, but another man is standing there.

This one is holding a knife. They both grab you and, with one dirty hand over your mouth, drag you towards the village port.

"This is where you get a choice," a deep voice says.

'Good,' you think. 'I can go home.' But that's not one of the choices offered.

"Two destinations; two ships. Both hunt whales. One's heading for the South Pacific Ocean, calling in on New Zealand and Australia. The other's heading for America. What will it be then, eh?"

*If you choose to go to the Pacific Ocean, **go to page 24**.*

*If you choose to go to America, **go to page 11**.*

JOURNEY LOG
Keep track of your adventures
to find every path and every ending.

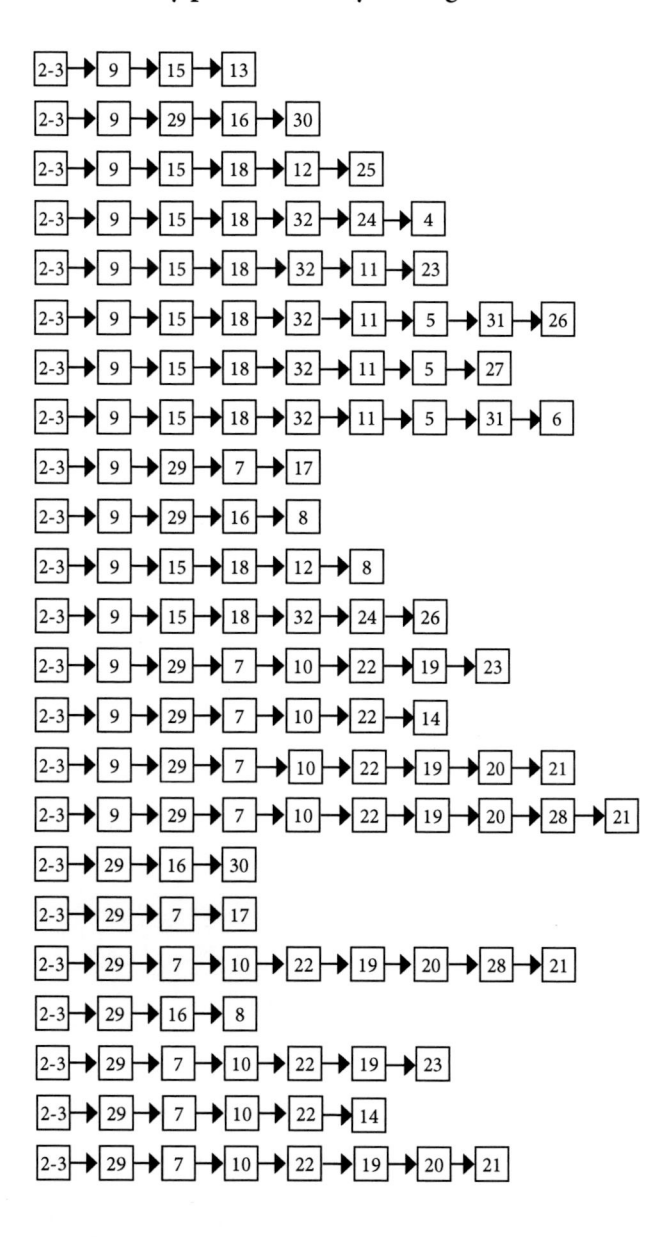

2-3 → 9 → 15 → 13

2-3 → 9 → 29 → 16 → 30

2-3 → 9 → 15 → 18 → 12 → 25

2-3 → 9 → 15 → 18 → 32 → 24 → 4

2-3 → 9 → 15 → 18 → 32 → 11 → 23

2-3 → 9 → 15 → 18 → 32 → 11 → 5 → 31 → 26

2-3 → 9 → 15 → 18 → 32 → 11 → 5 → 27

2-3 → 9 → 15 → 18 → 32 → 11 → 5 → 31 → 6

2-3 → 9 → 29 → 7 → 17

2-3 → 9 → 29 → 16 → 8

2-3 → 9 → 15 → 18 → 12 → 8

2-3 → 9 → 15 → 18 → 32 → 24 → 26

2-3 → 9 → 29 → 7 → 10 → 22 → 19 → 23

2-3 → 9 → 29 → 7 → 10 → 22 → 14

2-3 → 9 → 29 → 7 → 10 → 22 → 19 → 20 → 21

2-3 → 9 → 29 → 7 → 10 → 22 → 19 → 20 → 28 → 21

2-3 → 29 → 16 → 30

2-3 → 29 → 7 → 17

2-3 → 29 → 7 → 10 → 22 → 19 → 20 → 28 → 21

2-3 → 29 → 16 → 8

2-3 → 29 → 7 → 10 → 22 → 19 → 23

2-3 → 29 → 7 → 10 → 22 → 14

2-3 → 29 → 7 → 10 → 22 → 19 → 20 → 21

SPOT THE DIFFERENCE

Find 10 differences between the two illustrations on these pages.

(answers on activity disk and at www.chooseapathbooks.com)

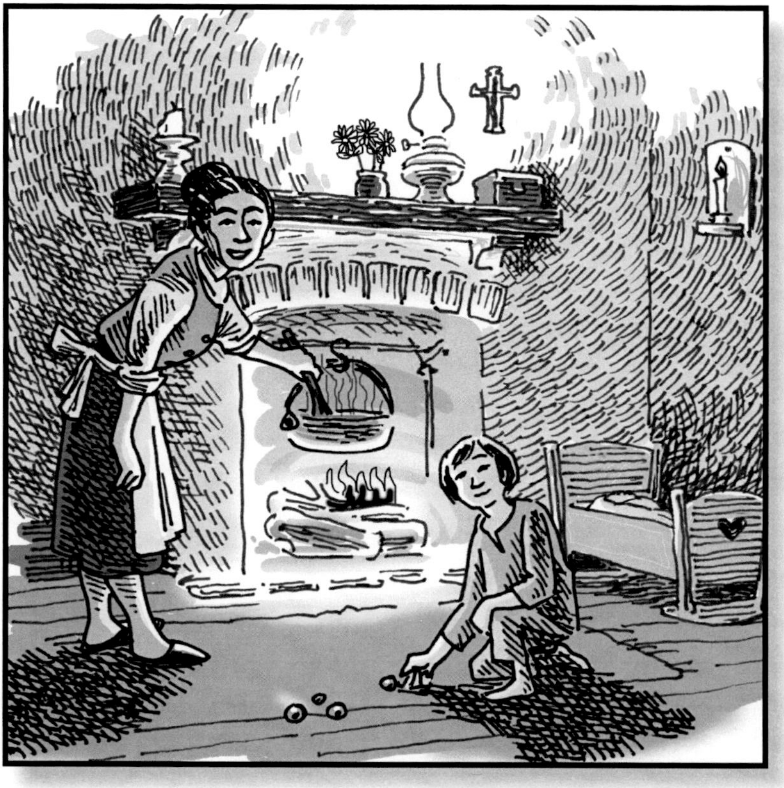

Choose A Path

12 PRINTABLE ACTIVITIES FOR EACH TITLE.
Available from www.www.chooseapathbooks.com

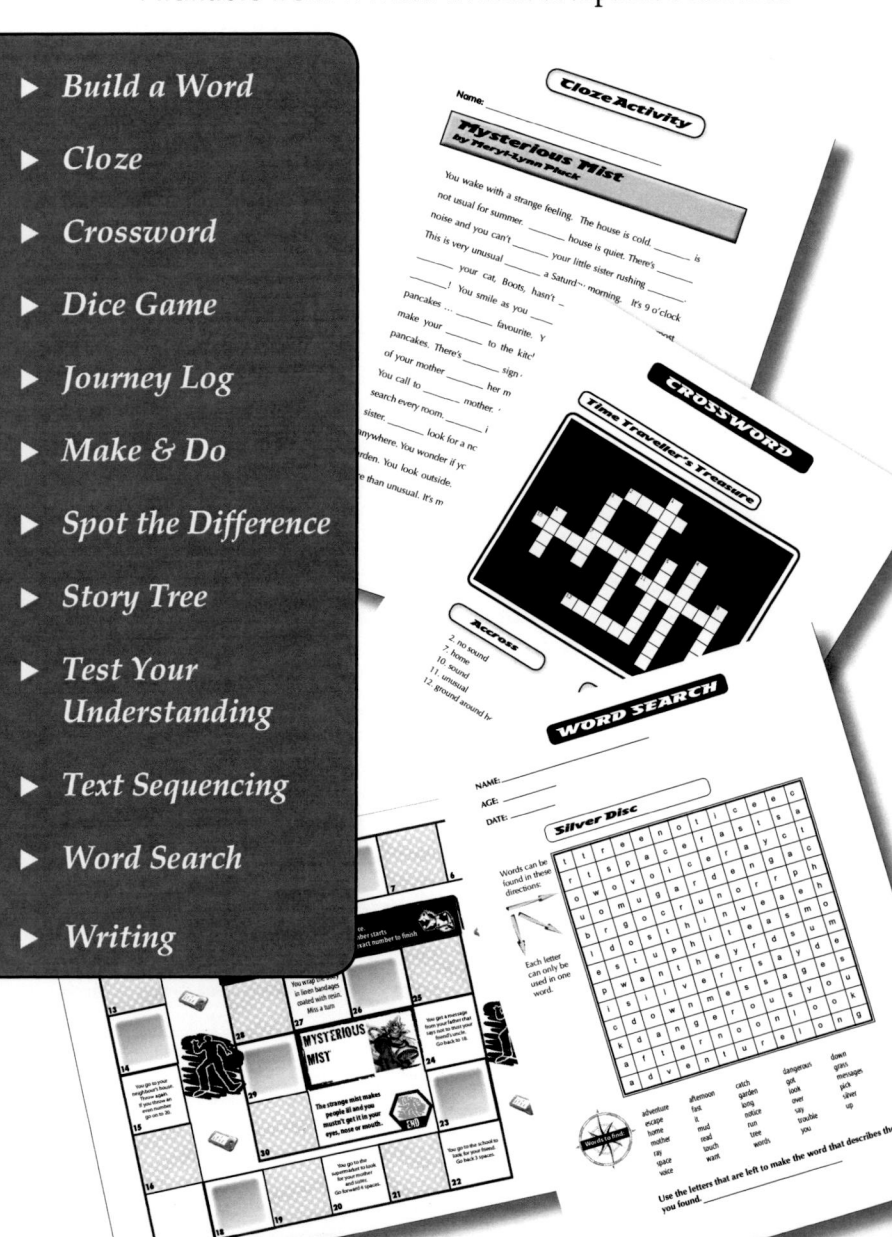

- ▶ **Build a Word**
- ▶ **Cloze**
- ▶ **Crossword**
- ▶ **Dice Game**
- ▶ **Journey Log**
- ▶ **Make & Do**
- ▶ **Spot the Difference**
- ▶ **Story Tree**
- ▶ **Test Your Understanding**
- ▶ **Text Sequencing**
- ▶ **Word Search**
- ▶ **Writing**

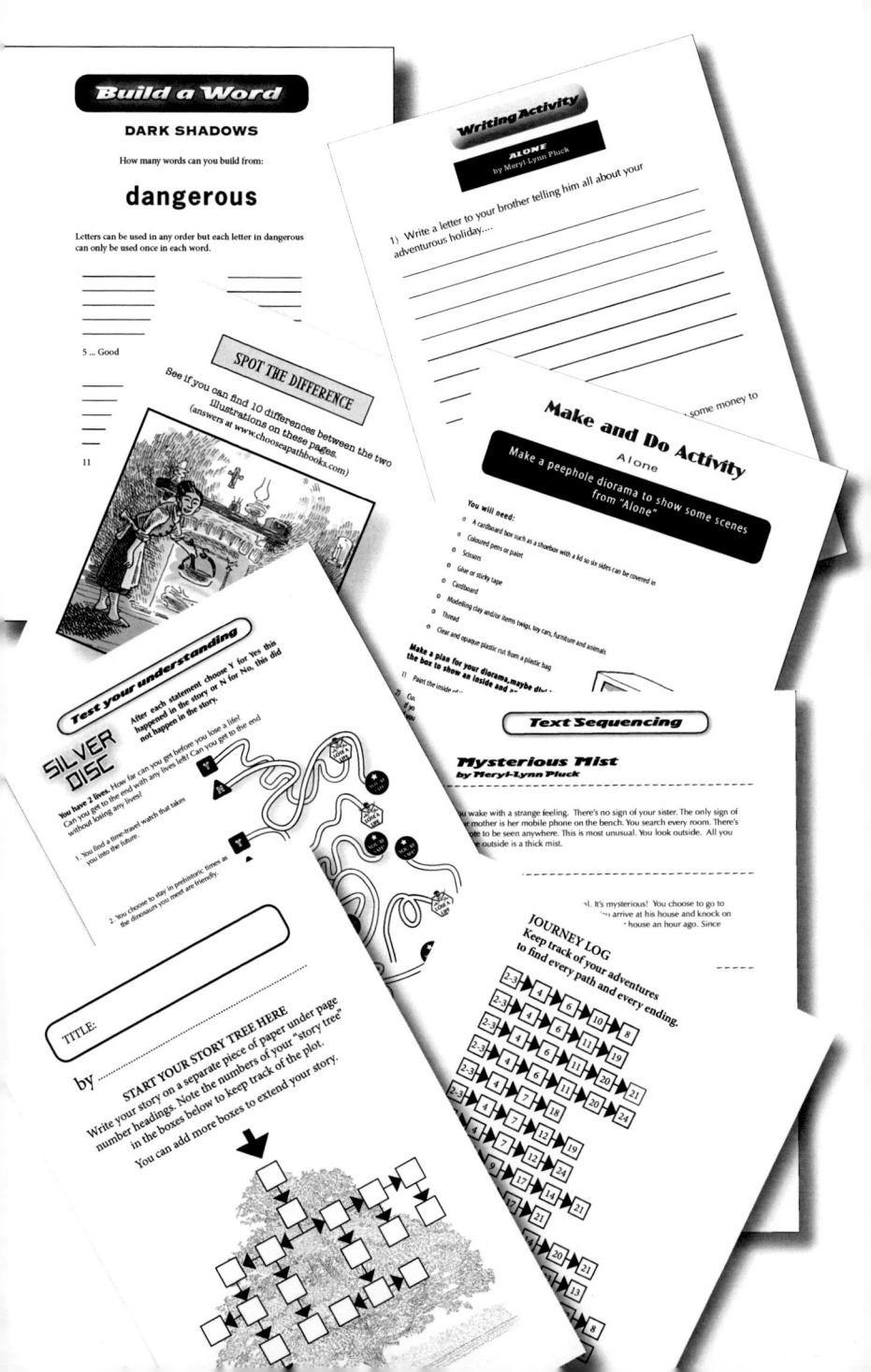

Build a Word

DARK SHADOWS

How many words can you build from:

dangerous

Letters can be used in any order but each letter in dangerous can only be used once in each word.

_____
_____
_____
_____
5 ... Good
_____
_____
_____
_____
11

SPOT THE DIFFERENCE

See if you can find 10 differences between the two illustrations on these pages.
(answers at www.chooseapathbooks.com)

Writing Activity

ALONE
by Meryl-Lynn Pluck

1) Write a letter to your brother telling him all about your adventurous holiday....

_____
_____
_____
_____
_____
_____

...some money to

Make and Do Activity

Alone

Make a peephole diorama to show some scenes from "Alone"

You will need:
- A cardboard box such as a shoebox with a lid so its sides can be covered in
- Coloured pens or paint
- Scissors
- Glue or sticky tape
- Cardboard
- Modelling clay and/or useful items twigs, toy cars, furniture and animals
- Thread
- Clear and opaque plastic cut from a plastic bag

Make a plan for your diorama, maybe draw the box to show an inside and s...

1) Paint the inside of...

Test your understanding

SILVER DISC

After each statement choose Y for Yes this happened in the story or N for No, this did not happen in the story.

You have 2 lives. How far can you get before you lose a life? Can you get to the end with any lives left? Can you get to the end without losing any lives?

1. You find a time-travel watch that takes you into the future.

2. You choose to stay in prehistoric times and the dinosaurs you meet are friendly.

Text Sequencing

Mysterious Mist
by Meryl-Lynn Pluck

You wake with a strange feeling. There's no sign of your sister. The only sign of ... mother is her mobile phone on the bench. You search every room. There's ... te to be seen anywhere. This is most unusual. You look outside. All you ... e outside is a thick mist.

... d. It's mysterious! You choose to go to ... arrive at his house and knock on ... house an hour ago. Since

---

JOURNEY LOG
Keep track of your adventures to find every path and every ending.

TITLE: _____

by ....

START YOUR STORY TREE HERE

Write your story on a separate piece of paper under page number headings. Note the numbers of your "story tree" in the boxes below to keep track of the plot. You can add more boxes to extend your story.

Other Choose A Path Titles in this Series...

ALONE

Meryl-Lynn Pluck

You're at home alone, bored and lonely. You decide it's time to make some new friends.

Should you choose to break a family rule by leaving the house without first checking with an adult?

Should you let a stranger into your house? Should you hang out with the wrong crowd at the school skate ramp? Should you steal food from a shop when you're hungry?

AVAILABLE FROM
www.chooseapathbooks.com

MYSTERIOUS MIST

MERYL-LYNN PLUCK

You wake one morning with a strange feeling. There's no sign of your mother or your sister and no note to be seen anywhere.

You look outside and see a strange thick mist. Should you choose to go out into the mist or stay home and seal the windows?

Should you choose to phone your father or check for news of the strange mist on the computer or TV?

SILVER DISC

Alison Condon

You're looking after your little sister Lisa when you see a silver disc lying on the ground. It's projecting words written in laser lights. "BEWARE! DO NOT TOUCH!" Should you choose to let Lisa pick it up? Should you give it back to the aliens who claim it is theirs? Should you put it into your computer?

TIME-TRAVELLER'S TREASURE

ALISON CONDON

You find some treasure and time-travel watches in your grandfather's basement. He tells you the watches shouldn't be touched as they're dangerous in the wrong hands. Should you choose to use the time-traveller's watches? Should you choose to stay and help your grandfather when he's threatened? When you find yourself back with dinosaurs in prehistoric times, should you get yourself to safety or save the treasure?